T0354442

Once upon a Christmas Miracle

When a pup finds a home for Christmas

Keiron Stringer

To order additional copies of this book, contact
Toll Free +65 3165 7531 (Singapore)
Toll Free +60 3 3099 4412 (Malaysia)
www.partridgepublishing.com/singapore
orders.singapore@partridgepublishing.com

Because of the dynamic nature of the Internet, any web addresses or links contained in this book may have changed since publication and may no longer be valid. The views expressed in this work are solely those of the author and do not necessarily reflect the views of the publisher, and the publisher hereby disclaims any responsibility for them.

ISBN
ISBN: 978-1-5437-8170-0 (sc)
ISBN: 978-1-5437-8169-4 (hc)
ISBN: 978-1-5437-8168-7 (e)

Library of Congress Control Number: 2024907135

Print information available on the last page.

09/16/2024

PARTRIDGE

Once upon a Christmas Miracle

Keiron Stringer

Bounty didn't know what to do.

Bounty saw a sign.
The nearest town was
30 miles away.

But she was so hungry and
cold, she decided to start
the long journey to town.

So Bounty kept on walking until she met a pig in the next field.

5

So bounty kept on walking and walking then she met a sheep on the way.

Bounty opened her eyes and saw a little girl. She was so happy, she forgot about her hunger and tiredness and stood up so happy wagging her tail.

It is a little puppy! You poor thing. I'm going to take you home and look after you

The girl took Bounty home and gave her a hot bath and some hot food.

Bounty got her Christmas miracle.
A home for Christmas.

Coming soon this October
Bounty's First Halloween

Printed in the United States
by Baker & Taylor Publisher Services